FACE-OFF

BY JAKE MADDOX

illustrated by Sean Tiffany

text by Anastasia Suen

Librarian Reviewer
Chris Kreie
Media Specialist, Eden Prairie Schools, MN
M.S. in Information Media, St. Cloud State University, MN

Reading Consultant
Mary Evenson
Middle School Teacher, Edina Public Schools, MN
M.A. in Education, University of Minnesota

▼▼ STONE ARCH BOOKS
Minneapolis   San Diego

Impact Books are published by Stone Arch Books,
151 Good Counsel Drive, P.O. Box 669,
Mankato, Minnesota 56002.
www.stonearchbooks.com

Library of Congress Cataloging-in-Publication Data
Maddox, Jake.
    Face-Off / by Jake Maddox; illustrated by Sean Tiffany.
    p. cm. — (Impact Books. A Jake Maddox Sports Story)
    Summary: Kyle wants to be a great hockey player just like his older
brother, but to do that, he must focus all of his energy on the game and
not be distracted by a teammate's injury.
    ISBN-13: 978-1-59889-063-1 (hardcover)
    ISBN-10: 1-59889-063-8 (hardcover)
    ISBN-13: 978-1-59889-237-6 (paperback)
    ISBN-10: 1-59889-237-1 (paperback)
    [1. Hockey—Fiction. 2. Teamwork (Sports)—Fiction.] I. Tiffany,
Sean, ill. II. Title. III. Series: Maddox, Jake. Impact Books (Stone Arch
Books) Jake Maddox Sports Story.
PZ7.S94343Fac 2007
[Fic]—dc22   2006006075

Art Director: Heather Kindseth
Cover Graphic Designer: Heather Kindseth
Interior Graphic Designer: Kay Fraser

1 2 3 4 5 6 11 10 09 08 07 06

Table of Contents

Chapter 1

EAGLES VS. ICE CATS

Kyle Parker sat on the bench as the hockey game was about to start. Eric, the Eagles' first-string center, was in the face off circle. Connor was his left wing, and Dave was his right wing.

The ref dropped the puck, and Eric slammed his stick down. The puck flew to Connor. The game had begun!

"I can't wait to get out there," said Kyle, watching the action on the rink.

"You and me both," said Sean, his best friend.

"Yeah," said Kyle. "I'd be out there scoring as left wing."

"It's not that easy," said Sean.

"It is for Parker boys," said Kyle. "Look at my brother, Caleb. He's the top scorer in the league."

"Kyle, Sean, Chris," said Coach Williams. "Out on the ice."

"About time," said Chris, the second line center.

Eric, Connor, and Dave came off the ice. Kyle, Sean, and Chris went in for their turn.

"Here we go," said Kyle.

The Ice Cats had scored.

The three new Eagles players all skated toward the face-off circle in the neutral zone.

Chris skated into the circle to wait for the face-off. He knew he had to get the puck to Sean, his right wing, before the other team got it.

The ref dropped the puck.

Chris hit the puck out of the circle. Sean skated over and caught it right on the tape. The Ice Cats' wings skated over to Sean, so he passed the puck to Kyle. Kyle moved the puck into the offensive zone.

The Ice Cats' left defenseman glided toward Kyle. He tried to knock the puck away. Kyle did a deke. He pretended to move right, but then he passed left to Sean.

Sean caught the puck on his stick and moved toward the goal. The goalie moved back and forth in front of the net.

Kyle moved around the Ice Cats' left defenseman toward Sean. Sean passed the puck to Chris. Chris spun around and passed the puck to Kyle.

I got this! Kyle thought. He aimed at the goal. The Ice Cats' defenseman swept the puck away from Kyle.

"Hey!" yelled Kyle. He spun around and chased the player, but it was too late. The Ice Cat player passed the puck to his center who was gliding quickly toward the Eagles' goal.

Kyle skated after the Ice Cats' center. So did Sean and Chris.

"Check, double check," said Sean.

"Let's do it," said Kyle.

Kyle skated up behind the Ice Cats' center. Kyle reached his stick out and lifted the Ice Cats' center's stick. Sean came in from the other side and stole the puck.

Sean passed the puck to Chris. Chris skated across the blue line into the offensive zone. Kyle followed Chris on the left. Chris passed the puck to Kyle.

Kyle got the puck. Then he snapped his wrist, and the puck flew through the air toward the net.

The goalie leaped.

Just when Kyle thought the puck was going in, the Ice Cats' goalie knocked the puck away with his glove.

SECOND SHIFT GOAL

Kyle sat on the bench as the second period was underway. The Eagles' players were skating around the Ice Cats' net.

"Look at that!" said Kyle. "Connor missed! How could he miss a shot like that?"

"Everyone misses sometime," said Sean.

"Not my brother, Caleb," said Kyle.

"I've seen him miss lots of times," said Sean.

"Yeah, but he scores a ton," said Kyle.

"Because he shoots a lot," said Sean.

"Kyle, Sean, Chris," said Coach Williams. "Out on the ice."

"Yes!" said Kyle. "Hey, Chris, hit it to me after the face off."

"You got it, man," said Chris. He skated into the face off circle in the neutral zone.

The ref dropped the puck and Chris slapped it out of the circle.

Here it comes, thought Kyle. He stopped the puck with his stick. Then he turned around and skated toward the offensive zone.

Kyle looked at the net. He saw an opening! He pulled his stick back and—wham! Slap shot!

The Ice Cats' goalie lifted his glove and caught the puck.

Man! Good save, thought Kyle.

"You should have waited until you were closer," said Chris as he skated past.

"Next time," said Kyle. "Hit it to me again."

"I'll try," said Chris.

On their next shift, Kyle's line won another face off. Kyle watched the puck fly toward him. I've got to score! he thought.

He glided closer to the net. The two Ice Cats' defensemen moved over to block the shot.

I can't shoot, Kyle thought.

He glanced at Sean. Sean looked open. Kyle figured that an assist was better than nothing!

Kyle moved his stick to sweep the puck over to Sean. Suddenly, an Ice Cat lifted Kyle's stick and stole the puck!

Kyle skated after the other player. He came from behind and lifted the Ice Cat's stick, stealing the puck back. Two can play this game! he said to himself.

Kyle spun around and skated back toward the net.

The defenseman was behind him, moving fast.

No time to waste, thought Kyle. There are only two players defending the goal.

Kyle swung his stick back.

Wham! Slap shot!

The puck sailed into the net.

The goalie missed!

I scored! thought Kyle. Oh yeah!

Chapter 3

BIG BROTHER

Kyle sat on the bench and looked out at the players on the ice. The Ice Cats had just scored on a power play. Their players outnumbered the Eagles on the ice five to four. They were now ahead of the Eagles for the second time that night.

"I'll never catch up with my brother's total by just sitting here," said Kyle.

"Look at that!" said Sean.

"Connor missed again. And Dave was a lot closer to the net."

"Connor doesn't like to share the puck," said Kyle.

"They're getting tired," said Sean.

"Yeah."

"Hey," said Sean. "Is that your brother over there?"

Caleb? Kyle looked up at the stands. "Where is he?" Caleb had never been to one of Kyle's games before. He was too busy playing center for the varsity team.

"That looks like him over there." Sean pointed.

Kyle tried to find his brother's face in the crowd. Then a whistle blew!

Coach Williams turned to the bench.

"Second line, get out there!" he said.

Kyle stood up and skated out onto the ice. There was no time to search for Caleb now. At least he'll get a chance to see me play, thought Kyle.

Chris and Sean skated out after him.

"Hit it my way, Chris," said Kyle.

"Go Eagles," said Chris, and he skated toward the face off circle.

An Ice Cat hit the puck after the drop.

"Oh no, you don't," said Kyle, and he skated after the puck. The Ice Cats' left wing had it, so Kyle lifted the wing's stick and swept it away.

Watch this, big brother, thought Kyle excitedly. I have the puck, and everyone else is behind me. Now I can score!

Suddenly, Kyle saw a flash of white. He was face down on the ice.

The ref grabbed the puck and skated to the scorer's area.

"Tripping!" called the ref. He turned to the Ice Cats' left wing and ordered him to the penalty box.

Kyle was brushing the ice off his jersey.

"He hooked me first!" said the wing, pointing at Kyle.

"Go to the box, Anderson," yelled the Ice Cats' coach.

"I'm going," said the Ice Cats' wing. As he skated away, he gave Kyle a dirty look.

It's your own fault, thought Kyle.

The ref looked at Kyle.

"You get a penalty shot, Parker,"
he said.

Yes! thought Kyle.

Kyle skated over to the center circle
where the ref had placed the puck.

Now's my chance, Kyle thought. No
one else is on the ice during a penalty
shot. It's just the goalie and me!

Kyle pushed off, and skated toward
the goal. He crossed the blue line.

Back and forth, Kyle pushed the puck
across the ice.

The Ice Cats' goalie stood near the
edge of the crease.

Kyle faked to the right, and the goalie
moved his body to the right too. Gotcha!
Kyle hit the puck left.

Goal!

Sean skated over to Kyle. "Sweet goal!" he said.

"I'll bet Caleb liked that," said Kyle.

"He left," said Sean. "I saw him walking out right after you got tripped. He was on crutches."

Chapter 4

BAD NEWS, GOOD ADVICE

That night, when Kyle got home, he ran to his brother's bedroom. Caleb's door was closed. It always was. Kyle could hear loud music playing on the other side.

Kyle knocked.

"The door's closed," came Caleb's voice. "That means no visitors!"

"It's me," yelled Kyle.

"No visitors means no visitors," Caleb yelled back.

Whatever, thought Kyle. He turned the doorknob and stepped inside.

"Hey!" said Caleb. "I thought I told you to stay out!"

"What happened?" asked Kyle. He was looking at his brother. Caleb was sitting up on his bed, watching TV. His right ankle was propped up on a pillow. There was a thick bandage wrapped around it.

"You broke your ankle!" said Kyle.

"I told you not to come in," said Caleb.

"How bad is it?" asked Kyle. "When can you get back on the ice?"

Caleb's eyes were angry. "Please, Kyle. I said, get out! Now!"

Kyle backed out of his brother's room. He closed the door just as Caleb threw a pillow at it from the other side.

In his own bedroom, Kyle lay down on the bed and stared at the ceiling.

What is Caleb going to do now? he wondered. The varsity team was important to him. He was the team's top scorer.

Kyle was about to turn off his bedside light when he heard a funny sound in the hall.

Stomp. Stomp.

Caleb appeared in the doorway. He had a crutch under his right arm.

"You got practice tomorrow?" asked the older brother.

"Yeah," said Kyle.

Caleb frowned. "Lower your shot."

"What?" Kyle asked.

"When you take your shot," said Caleb, "don't give the puck so much air."

"Cool," said Kyle.

Caleb turned and limped back to his bedroom.

Kyle turned off his light. He kept staring at the ceiling. He replayed the night's game in his head, over and over. Hit it lower, he told himself.

Chapter 5

EAGLES VS. COUGARS

The next week, the Eagles played at home against the Cougars.

"Eric, Dave, and Kyle, I want you out on the ice," said Coach Williams. "The game is about to start."

Wow! thought Kyle. I'm playing on the first line!

"But, Coach," said Connor, "that's my line."

"I'm going to mix it up this time," said Coach Williams.

Connor turned and glared at Kyle.

I scored two goals in the last game, thought Kyle as he skated out onto the ice. Connor didn't even have an assist.

"Hey, it's nice to have a Parker on the first line," said Eric as he skated to the center face off circle.

"Uh, thanks," said Kyle.

"Get ready to pass," said Dave, the right wing.

"You got it," said Kyle. He skated into position. It was time for the face off.

The Cougars' center skated into the face off circle. The ref looked at the clock. Then he nodded his head at the timekeeper.

"It's time, boys," the ref said. Then he dropped the puck.

Eric won the draw. Bam! The puck flew right. Dave received it right on the tape of his stick. The game was on!

Dave passed the puck back to Eric. Kyle, Dave, and Eric rushed over the blue line into the offensive zone.

Eric passed the puck to Kyle.

Oh yeah! thought Kyle. He moved closer to the goal. The Cougars' goalie backed into the crease. Kyle deked left and then passed the puck right to Eric. Eric blasted the puck into the net!

Goal!

The game just started, and I already have my first assist! thought Kyle.

He looked over at the bench.

Connor scowled at him. What? I'm supposed to play badly so you can get back on the ice? thought Kyle. No way!

"That was great," said Eric. "Let's do it again."

"Cool," said Kyle.

"Passing is how this line scores," said Dave.

On their next shift, Eric grabbed the puck on the face off and passed it to Kyle.

Here we go, thought Kyle.

The Eagles' first line passed the puck back and forth several times as they moved into the offensive zone. Finally, Kyle caught the pass from Eric.

This is my chance, thought Kyle.

He snapped his wrist. The puck flew toward the net.

The goalie threw his body onto the ice and blocked the puck

Man! I almost had it! thought Kyle. Maybe I should hit it lower next time, like Caleb said.

He turned back toward the bench. Connor was smiling. Kyle couldn't understand why. He's happy because I was blocked? wondered Kyle.

Coach Williams called for a line change.

"You think you're cool, don't you?" said Connor as he came out onto the ice. "Just because you're a Parker. But you're big brother isn't so hot anymore with a broken ankle, is he?"

Chapter 6

PULL OUT

Kyle was angry. He had wanted to punch Connor, but he controlled himself. Getting into a fight wouldn't help him or the team. It wouldn't help his brother, either.

After a few more shifts, the coach called out the first line again.

Kyle looked up at the clock. The third period was almost over!

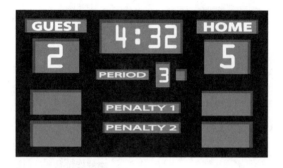

We're ahead five to two, he thought.

Eric won the face off. Then Dave skated over and got the puck.

As long as Kyle was playing, he could forget about being angry at Connor.

The first line rushed into the Cougars' zone. Eric passed the puck to Kyle.

Yes! I see a hole! thought Kyle.

Kyle fired the puck toward the net. The goalie reached out his blocker, and the puck bounced back out. Eric came in for the rebound. He slid the puck past the goalie. Goal!

The score was six to two. The Eagles were ahead.

At the next face off, Eric was overpowered by the Cougars' center. The center caught the puck and rushed toward the Eagles' net.

Kyle raced to catch up with him.

Smoothly, the Cougars' line moved the puck back and forth between them.

We must be getting tired, thought Kyle, or the Cougars are getting stronger.

Dave tried to steal the puck, but the Cougars' wing kept it under control.

Closer and closer the Cougars skated toward the net. The Eagles' two defensemen moved in front of the goal.

A Cougar pulled his stick back. Slap shot! He scored.

BZZZ! The buzzer sounded. The game was over with a score of six to three. The Cougars had made another goal, but the Eagles still won.

Eric skated around the ice with his stick in the air. Kyle skated over to give him a high five. Whap! Their gloves slapped in the air.

"I want Coach to make you part of our line," said Eric.

"We never scored this many points with Connor," said Dave.

"I heard that," said Connor. Kyle turned around. "You can't replace me," said Connor. "I'm not going to sit on the bench anymore!"

Chapter 7

SEAN'S PROBLEM

A week later, the Eagles were hosting the Archers. As the Eagles sat on the bench, Coach Williams looked up from his clipboard. "First line," he said.

Eric, Kyle, and Dave stood up and climbed over the boards.

"But Coach," said Connor.

"You played with Sean and Chris all week during practice," said Coach, "and it worked out just fine."

"He hogs the puck the whole time," muttered Sean.

"Then don't pass it to him," Dave whispered back to him.

"Yeah, right," said Sean.

As he skated toward the face off circle, Eric said to Kyle, "Now our line is solid."

"It was six to three last week," said Dave. "Let's see if we can top that."

"No problem," said Kyle.

The Archers' first line was waiting for them at center ice. When the ref dropped the puck, the Archers' center pulled it back for his defenseman. Then the Archers' line skated toward the Eagles' zone.

"Where's the defense?" yelled Eric.

An Archers' wing rocketed over to the Eagles' net. The center set him up for a nice slap shot! Goal!

"Come on, men!" said Eric as he glided past Kyle. "Let's get it together."

The Archers won the next face off, too. This time, Dave spun around and stole the puck.

"Kyle!" he shouted.

Dave slipped the puck sideways to Kyle. Kyle caught it right on the tape.

Let's do this, he told himself.

Kyle skated toward the goal with Dave and Eric at his side.

Kyle saw a gap on the right side of the net. He passed the puck to Dave. The goalie shifted his position, and Dave slipped the puck back to Kyle.

Hit it hard and low! thought Kyle. He snapped his wrist.

Bam! The puck slammed the back of the net.

Cool! A goal for me and an assist for Dave, thought Kyle. Maybe I will catch up with Caleb!

Coach Williams waved them in.

Kyle skated toward the bench. "Hey," said Kyle as Sean skated past, but Sean didn't even look at him.

What's his problem? Kyle turned around and watched as Sean skated over to the face off circle.

Then Chris skated past Kyle without saying a word.

Connor shoved his face up to Kyle's.

"You can't take my place," said Connor. "I'm a better player than you are." Then he skated off.

Kyle skated back to the bench. I'm helping the team win, he thought. Why is everyone mad at me?

Chapter 8

UPSET

The second period was about to start. Kyle skated onto the ice as the first line took their positions.

"It's so cool we're not playing with Connor anymore," said Eric.

"He hogs the puck the whole time anyway," said Dave.

"Sean's upset about it," said Kyle.

"Better him than me," said Dave.

Wham! Eric hit the puck out to Kyle.

Wow, Eric is really good, thought Kyle. He's a better stickhandler than Chris ever was.

Kyle caught the puck from Eric's shot and skated toward the goal.

Bam! An Archers' player slid up next to him and stole his puck.

I didn't even see that guy, thought Kyle. He glanced over at the coach, who was signaling him to keep his eyes open. Just behind the coach was Sean. Sean wasn't even watching the game

It's not my fault I'm on the first line and Sean isn't, thought Kyle.

Kyle stopped thinking about Connor, Sean, and Chris. He put his mind completely on the game.

Swoosh! Dave flew in and stole the puck from the Archers' wing. He passed the puck to Eric. Eric slid it over to Kyle.

Kyle knew Eric was closer to the goal, so Kyle passed the puck back to Eric.

One of the Archers' defensemen swept his stick at the puck as Eric skated by.

The puck skidded across the ice.

Kyle skated after it and the Archers' players surrounded him.

"Get out of there, Kyle!"

Who shouted that? thought Kyle. It wasn't Sean or Coach Williams.

The Archers' center now had the puck. Kyle poke-checked the puck free. Dave picked up the puck and passed it back to Kyle.

Kyle spun around and sprinted toward the goal. He was on a breakaway!

All of the Archers' forwards skated after him. Kyle could hear their blades scraping the ice behind him, getting closer and closer.

Suddenly Kyle's foot got stuck. He fell forward onto the ice. "Tripping!" called the ref.

"I didn't trip him," said the Archers' center.

"Your stick is under his body," said the ref as Kyle picked himself up. "And he was in front of you. That makes it tripping."

"I don't believe this!" said the Archers' center.

"You want more time in the box?" asked the ref.

"Watch yourself next time," the center muttered to Kyle as he glided off.

The ref turned to Kyle and said, "You get a penalty shot."

Kyle nodded. He skated over to the center of the ice.

The ref set the puck. Kyle tapped it with his stick and began moving toward the goal.

This was how I made it to first string, thought Kyle. It was that breakaway that showed Coach I was good enough.

"Do it, Kyle!"

That voice again. Kyle looked over at the stands. It was Caleb, with a few of his buddies.

Caleb was standing up, holding on to his crutch, and waving his hand.

This time he's not leaving the game, thought Kyle.

The Archer's goalie backed into the crease as Kyle glided closer and closer.

The goalie's eyes moved back and forth, watching the puck.

Kyle searched for an opening. A small gap opened between the goalie's left skate and the net.

That was all Kyle needed.

Kyle took a deep breath. Hit it low, he told himself, remembering what his brother had said.

Whap!

Kyle hit the puck as hard as he could.

Nice and low.

The puck blasted past the goalie's skates and right into the back of the net.

Goal!

Caleb was holding his crutch over his head, waving it back and forth.

Chapter 9

BLOOD ON THE ICE

Kyle skated into position near the face-off circle. The game was almost over.

Eric and Dave coasted into place.

Kyle looked up at the scoreboard. Eagles 7, Archers 6. He had scored two of those goals himself. He also had three assists. One more goal and he would catch up with Caleb's totals for the season.

The Eagles won the next face off.

Dave caught the puck and started skating toward the goal. Kyle and Eric followed. So did all of the Archers' forwards.

Kyle skated over to Dave's left. But before Dave could pass the puck, Kyle saw the Archers' center reach his stick out.

"Dave!" yelled Kyle. Too late. Dave tripped over the center's stick and tumbled face down onto the ice.

Kyle skated over and touched Dave's arm. Then he saw Dave's forehead.

"He's bleeding!" said Kyle.

Connor was mad. He came charging onto the ice, ready to start a fight.

Both benches emptied as players came out onto the ice. Sean grabbed Connor's arm. "Stop it, man!"

"You're not helping!" said Eric as he grabbed Connor's other arm.

Coach Williams and the Archers' coach ran over. "Back to the bench, Connor!" said Coach Williams.

"But—" said Connor.

"Make that the locker room," said the ref. "You're out of the game."

Connor stormed off the ice.

The ref turned to look at the Archers' center. "You're out too."

The Archers' center looked over at the bench. His coach pointed to the locker room.

Kyle moved aside so Coach Williams could look at Dave.

"Can you hear me, Dave?" asked Coach Williams.

Finally, Dave opened his eyes.

"Don't get up yet, son," said Coach Williams. He held up two fingers. "How many fingers do you see?"

"Uh, three," said Dave. "No, four."

"I think he has a concussion," said Coach Williams. "Help me carry him off the ice. His mom will need to take him to the doctor."

"Let me help," said the Archers' coach. The two coaches lifted Dave up slowly. They held on to the boy as he tried to stand up.

"Lean on me," said Coach Williams. The two coaches helped Dave off the ice. Dave's mom was waiting there.

Coach Williams spoke with Dave's mom.

Caleb and his buddies had come down from the stands and were standing close by the Eagles' bench.

"We can help, Coach!" said Caleb's friend Andy. Andy and his buddy helped Dave walk out of the arena. Dave's mom walked by their side.

Kyle wondered what would happen next.

Chapter 10

LAST PLAY

Ten minutes passed, and the Eagles' players were still waiting for the game to start again. Caleb turned to his brother. "Dave will be fine," he said. "It's time to get your head back in the game."

"This stinks," said Kyle. "Dave gets hurt, and Connor and Sean are mad at me because I'm on the first line."

"That's their problem," said Caleb. "Just ignore it. You got there because you're good."

"Yeah," said Kyle. "Thanks."

The players turned around as the two coaches and Caleb's buddies came back inside the arena.

"Will Dave be all right?" asked Kyle.

"He was talking in the car," said Coach Williams, "so he'll be fine. He just needs to be checked out by a doctor."

"We can go and see him tomorrow," said Sean.

Kyle turned around and looked at Sean. "We can both go tomorrow."

"But first we have to finish this game," said Coach Williams.

"Sean plays right wing," he said. "Okay, boys. Let's finish what we started."

Sean looked at Kyle and smiled.

The new first line skated out onto the ice. Eric skated into the face off circle. Kyle and Sean took their places.

"We both got our wish, huh?" said Kyle.

"Yup, first line," said Sean.

The ref skated out with the puck and dropped it. Eric hit it out and Sean caught it.

Sean skated toward the goal and passed the puck to Eric. Eric skated into the offensive zone and passed the puck to Kyle.

Kyle hit the puck as hard as he could!

The puck sailed right between the goalie's legs.

BZZZ! The game was over.

"Hat trick!" yelled Sean. "You got a hat trick!"

Eric skated over and gave Kyle a high five. "Three goals in one game!" Hats came flying onto the ice.

Sean slapped Kyle a high five too.

Kyle skated near the bench where Caleb was watching the game.

"You know how to play a good game, little brother," said Caleb.

"I have to," replied Kyle. "I'm a Parker boy, right?"

About the Author

Anastasia Suen is the author of more than seventy books for young people. Her children spent many years playing street hockey in front of their house. Anastasia grew up in Florida and now lives with her family in Plano, Texas.

About the Illustrator

When Sean Tiffany was growing up, he lived on a small island off the coast of Maine. Every day, from sixth grade until he graduated from high school, he had to take a boat to get to school. When Sean isn't working on his art, he works on a multimedia project called "OilCan Drive," which combines music and art. He has a pet cactus named Jim.

Glossary

assist (uh-SIST)—help make a goal

breakaway (BRAYK-uh-way)—when the player with the puck is in front of the other players as he moves toward the goal

concussion (kuhn-KUSH-uhn)—an injury to the brain caused by a heavy blow to the head

deke (deek)—a false move, or "decoy," to trick your opponent

hat trick (hat trik)—three goals scored by a player in one game

lunge (luhnj)—move forward quickly and suddenly

penalty (PEN-uhl-tee)—punishment for breaking the rules

power play (POW-ur play)—when one team has more players on the ice than the other team, because the other team has a player out because of a penalty

Further Info

Here are some more hockey definitions. Try writing a short story that includes all of these words!

1 **Central Ice**—this is the central face-off spot, where the first face-off in a game of hockey takes place

2 **Neutral Face Off Spots**—these face-off circles take place in the middle, or neutral, zone of a hockey rink

3 **End Zone Face Off Spots**—these four circles are in the two end zones. A team calls the zone with their goal the "defending zone."

Other Hockey Terms

crease (KREESS)—the rounded area outside the goal. The crease gives a goalie room to defend his goal without interference.

blocker (BLOK-uhr)—a long flat glove with a board inside, which is worn by the goalie

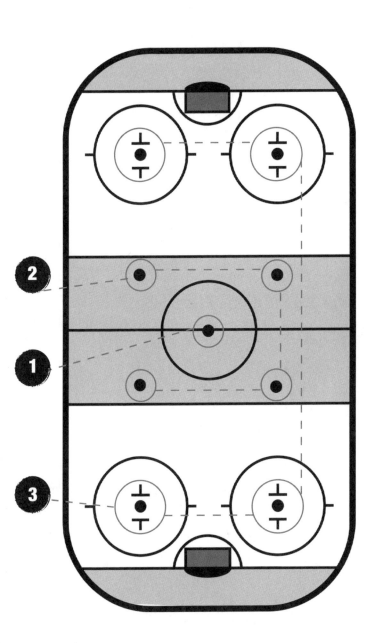

Discussion Questions

1. Why does the main character, Kyle, want to match his brother's scoring total?

2. Why do you think the character Connor "hogs" the puck?

3. Why was Sean mad at Kyle?

Writing Prompts

1. What would you do if you had to play second string and sit on the bench?

2. How would you feel if your best friend got promoted to first string and you didn't?

3. What do you think happened in the next game?

Internet Sites

Do you want to know more about subjects related to this book? Or are you interested in learning about other topics? Then check out FactHound, a fun, easy way to find Internet sites.

Our investigative staff has already sniffed out great sites for you!

Here's how to use FactHound:

1. Visit *www.facthound.com*

2. Select your grade level.

3. To learn more about subjects related to this book, type in the book's ISBN number: **1598890638**.

4. Click the **Fetch It** button.

FactHound will fetch the best Internet sites for you!